Sylvain Trudel

Max the Superhero

Illustrations by Suzanne Langlois

Translated by Sarah Cummins

Formac Publishing Company Limited
Halifax, Nova Scotia 1996

Originally published as Le garçon qui rêvait d'être un héros.

Canadian Cataloguing in Publication Data

Trudel, Sylvain, 1963–

[Garçon qui rêvait d'être un héros. English]

Max the superhero

(First novel series)

Translation of: Le garçon qui rêvait d'être un héros.

ISBN 0-88780-376-8 (pbk.) — ISBN 0-88780-377-6 (bound)

I. Langlois, Suzanne II. Title. III. Title: Garçon qui rêvait d'être un héros. English. IV. Series.

PS8589.R719G3713 1996 jC843'.54 C96-950102-3
PZ7.T78Ma 1996

Formac Publishing Limited
5502 Atlantic Street
Halifax, N.S. B3H 1G4

Printed and bound in Canada

Contents

1
A good thing I'm here

My name is Max and I dream a lot about saving everyone in the whole world.

You might not realize it, but there are a lot of people to save. Lost children, the homeless and the poor, sick babies and sad people.

Sometimes on Sunday my aunts and uncles come over for a visit. They always ask me, "What do you want to be, Max, when you grow up?"

They expect me to say "an astronaut" or "a fireman" or "a hockey player." But I don't answer.

I wish I could say, "When I grow up, I'm going to be a hero." I don't say anything, because grown-ups don't take heroes seriously. Once when I told them that I wanted to be a hero, they all burst out laughing. Ever since, I have kept my secret like a little jewel.

People who save the world are heroes. Everyone loves them. But they do have enemies — enemies who come from the cosmos.

There have to be enemies because without them there would be no combat. And heroes love combat. It's what they live for!

Like everyone else, I have my own heroes.

My favourite hero is the Flying Avenger. He flies through the skies. He is strong and kind. Every Thursday evening, he saves the world. Girls love him. He even vanquished the Giant Grasshopper that was trying to devour the earth!

The Flying Avenger wears a red cape, a silver mask, and jet boots. He has a magic ring which gives him strength and courage. When he flies through the clouds, his cape turns incredibly beautiful and shimmery.

Sometimes the Flying Avenger has to fight Lava Man.

Lava Man is a monster who lives in volcanoes and spits fire onto houses nearby. Once, the Flying Avenger doused Lava Man by throwing a whole ocean on him.

The Evil Chimera is another one of the Flying Avenger's enemies. She has the claws of a lion, the head of a crocodile, the body of a porcupine, and the tail of a dragon.

All kinds of terrible creatures want to destroy the world: the Venimous Mole, the Screaming Spider, the Electric Octopus, and a whole lot more! But the Flying Avenger is here to save us.

Every Thursday I hurry to the newspaper stand. I buy my favourite comic, *The Adventures of the Flying Avenger*. As soon as I have it in my trembling hands, I skim through it.

What will happen this time? Who will attack the Earth? Will the Flying Avenger save us?

At night, when I start worrying about the end of the world, I breathe on my bedroom window. In the mist from my breath, I draw galaxies. I think about the Flying Avenger, and then I'm not so scared. I look at the lights of the city and I think, "Each light is someone's life. And every one of these lights must be protected."

I think about my parents, asleep in their bedroom. I think about my two little sisters, Zoë and Thea. I feel sure that monsters are trying to break into our house.

But I will protect my family. I'll fight for them.

Today is November 24th. Outside it is dark and cold. The wind is blowing hard. It sounds like the cries of lost children.

I hide under my covers and imagine that I am flying through the sky like a shining meteor. I have a silver mask, jet boots, a magic ring, and a shimmery red cape.

I am the Flying Avenger and I protect my family against monsters. My mission is to save those I love.

It's a good thing I'm here.

2
In one month—Christmas!

The next morning at school, Mrs. Atkins told us, "Today is November 25th. In one month, it will be Christmas."

Yippee! The whole class shouted in excitement. I looked over at my best friend Ben and I could see stars dancing in his eyes. He was grinning in delight.

Last year Ben used to read *The Adventures of the Flying Avenger* too. But this year he likes to read *Car Crazy*, a magazine about model cars.

Everyone was excited thinking about their favourite toys.

Mrs. Atkins asked us to please calm down, and then she became very serious. We could tell she wanted to tell us about something important.

"I suggest that this year our class should make Christmas baskets for poor families."

Silence fell over the classroom. Even Julie, who usually chatters like a magpie, was silent. We thought about the poor people, with Christmas coming. It was sad.

Poor people never have much of a Christmas. It really isn't fair.

"What do you think?" asked Mrs. Atkins.

We all agreed that it was a very good idea. We would put together beautiful Christmas baskets for the poor. They deserve presents too.

"That's great," said Mrs. Atkins. "Now please get out your math books."

We started on our multiplication tables.

During recess we talked about poor people and their Christmases. Our friend Laura told us something unbelievable.

"When my grandfather was a kid, he got nothing for Christmas but an orange."

"An orange? Nothing but an orange!?" we all cried.

"Weren't there any models to build?" asked Ben.

"Of course not!" answered Laura. "This was in the olden days."

Ben looked horrified. He couldn't imagine Christmas without the aircraft carrier model he had seen in the store. He dreamed about it night and day.

Then Ben turned to me. "Hey! Did I tell you I saw a Flying Avenger costume?"

"What? A Flying Avenger costume? Where?"

"At the toy store! I saw it last night and I thought of you! It's the real thing!"

I was so happy I almost died. A real Flying Avenger costume! It was exactly what I wanted!

I had trouble concentrating in class for the rest of the day. When Mrs. Atkins asked me, "How much is five times three?" I answered, "Eight."

All the other kids laughed,

because the right answer is fifteen. I had added instead of multiplying. Then later, in science, Mrs. Atkins asked me another question.

"What is the name of the small mammal that digs long tunnels under the earth?"

I answered, "The Venimous Mole."

Everyone laughed again, even Mrs. Atkins, which doesn't happen very often. I was thinking about the adventures of the Flying Avenger and just said whatever popped into my head.

"I hope you will get lots of rest this weekend," Mrs. Atkins told me.

After school I ran to the toy store in the mall. My heart was thumping. As I rounded the cor-

ner I saw the genuine Flying Avenger costume!

It was all there: the silver mask, the jet boots, the magic ring, and the red cape.

I couldn't wait for Christmas to come!

3
Disaster strikes

That evening at dinner something weird happened. When we sat down at the table, there was nothing to eat but spaghetti — with no sauce. We sat and stared at our plates. My mother raised her head and asked, "Why aren't you eating? Aren't you hungry?"

My sisters and I looked at each other in bewilderment. Since I'm the oldest one, I spoke up.

"But Mom ... we're waiting for the meat sauce."

Spaghetti without meat sauce is not the same — just pale, soft, watery-tasting noodles.

"Eat up and don't ask any questions!" shouted my father grumpily.

So we ate our spaghetti without asking any questions. We put salt on it, but it still wasn't very good.

We wanted to have ice cream for dessert, but there wasn't any left.

"How come there's no ice cream?" I asked my mother.

"There wasn't any more at the store," she replied.

That was a very strange answer, but I didn't say anything. My dad was glaring at me.

Then we wanted to have some chocolate-chip cookies, but the bag was empty.

"Why didn't you buy any cookies?"

It was so weird! There was hardly anything to eat! I thought of delicious sugar donuts.

"How come you didn't buy any donuts?"

Then my dad got really mad. He jumped up from his chair and grabbed me by the arm. He dragged me to my room like an old sack of potatoes. The look on his face was terrifying and he was yelling.

Zoë and Thea started to cry. Mom told them to stop it right away. My dad was furious.

"I don't want you to set foot out of this room until tomorrow morning! That will teach you to think about food all the time!"

He slammed the door and I lay down on my bed and started to cry. I couldn't understand why he had pulled my arm so hard.

After a little while I got out my Flying Avenger comics. Looking at them again I noticed that when monsters attack the Earth, people are filled with terror. My dad's eyes looked like the eyes of these frightened people.

"Dad must be afraid of the end of the world, just like the people in the comics. That's

why he grabbed my arm. He didn't realize what he was doing. It must be his nerves."

Before falling asleep, I breathed mist on the window and drew galaxies. I looked far out into the starry night. I was looking for my hero, the Flying Avenger.

He always leaves a shining trail behind him when he flies through the sky. It looks like a shooting star. But I didn't see anything.

Suddenly I thought I saw a shadow slipping through the laneway!

Maybe it was the Atomic Cobra! Or the Bloodsucking Toad! I leaped back into bed and buried myself under the covers.

"I must protect my poor parents and my little sisters. I *have* to have the Flying Avenger costume."

4
The Christmas baskets

I thought that things would get better, but they didn't. There were still no cookies in the pantry. No ice cream in the freezer. No meat sauce on our spaghetti.

One morning I scraped my spoon on the bottom of the jar of strawberry jam. It made a sad little sound, the music of no more jam. There were no other jars of strawberry jam.

Before leaving for school, I went to find my mother.

"Mrs. Atkins asked us to bring in canned foods today. We're

making up our Christmas baskets for the poor people."

My mother got a funny look on her face, but she opened the cupboard door and gave me the last can of sardines.

When I caught up with Ben, I saw that he had a bag full of cans. Soup, ravioli, fruit salad, stew, all kinds of things!

I felt sad.

"Could you give me two or three cans?" I asked him. "I'll trade you for some hockey cards."

"How come you want some of my cans?"

I looked at my sardines and murmured, "I'm ashamed. One can of sardines isn't enough. What would it look like, next to all your stuff?"

Ben reached into his bag and

handed me his ravioli, his pears, and his chicken noodle soup.

"You can keep your hockey cards, Max."

Ben is a true friend. Thanks to him, I didn't need to feel ashamed.

We all piled up our cans in the

classroom. It made a mountain of food! Mrs. Atkins was proud of us, and we were happy for the poor people.

We spent all morning putting the Christmas baskets together. We called them “baskets” because it sounds nicer, but really they were cardboard boxes. We put cans of food in each one, with a card wishing the recipients the best of the season.

The boxes had already been used for Florida oranges, which made me think of the children in olden times who only got an orange for Christmas. I wondered if they were happy with that.

I hope I get the Flying Avenger costume for Christmas. I’m glad I don’t live in the olden days.

This afternoon, like every Thursday afternoon, I'll go buy my Flying Avenger comic. I wonder who will attack the Earth today. Maybe the Blazing Coyote or Metal Jaws. Or maybe the Lunatic Skeleton.

It makes me shiver just to think about it ...

5
Lies

On Tuesday morning my friend Ben had a funny look on his face. He told me he wanted to tell me a secret. I was intrigued.

Ben whispered in my ear, "Yesterday I had to go to the dentist at the mall. I saw a man sitting on one of the benches ... someone you know ..."

"Someone I know? Who?"

"Well, it was ... uh, your father."

"My father? But that's impossible! My father works in an office downtown! He goes off to work every morning!"

"Max, I'm telling you I saw your dad at the mall."

"I don't believe you. It can't be. You made a mistake."

At noon, instead of going home for lunch, Ben and I went to the mall. Ben walked in front of me. I hid behind him so as not to be seen. We explored every corner of the mall.

Suddenly my heart stopped. I saw my dad sitting on a bench. He was staring off into space. It was him all right, but he looked like someone else. All alone, like an outcast. He looked depressed. I was afraid.

"Come on! Let's get out of here!'

We left. I was devastated. I didn't get any work done at school. All afternoon, I kept thinking of my poor dad.

He came home that evening around six, as usual. He hugged us. I acted like everything was normal.

"Hi, Dad. Did you have a good day at the office?"

He shot a look at my mother before answering.

"Yes. How about you? Have a good day at school?"

I nodded my head, but I felt like this was the worst day of my life. The evening was just as bad. I couldn't concentrate on my homework. I kept thinking of how my dad had lied.

He obviously wanted me to think he was still working. But really he had lost his job. And without a job, you don't earn any money.

Without money, you can't have ice cream or cookies. You can't put meat sauce on your spaghetti. Sometimes you don't even have a house, or a car, or warm clothes.

And you don't have any Christmas presents either.

The next day I told Ben my painful secret.

"Don't tell anyone else, but I think my family is poor now."

Poverty was like a monster that had come down from the sky to attack my family. I wished I were the Flying Avenger.

6
No dreams

Then a miracle happened! On Monday there was food in the pantry and the refrigerator!

Peanut butter, jam, juice, bananas, sugar donuts ... even a jar of meat sauce for our spaghetti!

We were hungry and we had food to eat. I thought we were saved.

"Next week, we'll have a wonderful Christmas!"

But when I went to get my hockey stick out of the shed, I realized that we were not saved. I saw three empty boxes at the back of the shed.

Three boxes that had once been used to transport oranges from Florida ...

So my parents had received Christmas baskets! That explained why there was food in the house. That night in bed, I told myself, "I'm poor. I'm poor. I'm poor ..."

I couldn't really believe it but, by repeating it over and over, I finally managed to convince myself. I fell asleep poor and I didn't have any dreams.

The next day I went back to the mall at lunchtime just to

make sure. I saw my father sitting on a bench again.

He looked twice as depressed as he had the previous week. I ran away as fast as I could.

I had always thought that poor people lived in poor neighbourhoods. But any neighbourhood in the world can turn into a poor neighbourhood.

Any house can be a house where poor people live.

Any galaxy can be a galaxy of poor people. Even the Flying Avenger's galaxy.

7
A little Christmas

It was the last day of school before the Christmas holidays. After school, my friends wanted to go over to the mall. There were lots of fun games to play there.

At first I didn't want to go with them. I was afraid we'd run into my father. And anyway, I didn't have any money. But Ben insisted.

"Come on, Max! Come with us! It's Christmas. I'll treat you."

I hesitated, but finally I went along. It turned out okay

because I didn't see my dad there.

We had a lot of fun, my friends and I. We played pinball and went bowling and we rode the little train around.

I went over to the toy shop. The Flying Avenger costume was still on display. I felt sad.

At the far end of the mall was a little village covered with snow made of cotton wool. Santa Claus was seated on his throne, next to the Queen of the Fairies.

"Let's go see Santa! Come on, it'll be fun!"

When my turn came, I went and sat on Santa's knee. I could see my friends all laughing, but I was very serious.

I had a sad lump in my throat.

Santa Claus lowered his eyes, as if he was shy. But he boomed out, "Ho! Ho! Ho! And what is your name?"

"Max."

"Ho! Ho! Ho! Have you been a good boy, Max?"

I nodded my head yes, but I wanted to tell him something else. It was hard.

"Santa Claus," I sighed, "I have a secret to tell you. In my family, we're poor. I could have asked you for the Flying Avenger costume, but I don't want a present. All I want is enough for us to eat."

Santa Claus kept his eyes down and didn't say anything.

"I just want a little Christmas," I added.

The Queen of the Fairies gave

me a lollipop. I knew it was time to let another kid talk to Santa. I went back to my friends.

"What did you ask him for? What do you want for Christmas?"

"I asked him for meat sauce to put on our spaghetti."

My friends all laughed their heads off. They split their sides laughing. They thought it was a very funny joke. Only Ben didn't smile.

8
December 25th

On Christmas morning, my little sisters Zoë and Thea came in to wake me up.

"Get up! It's Christmas! Christmas is here!"

I rubbed my eyes and got out of bed.

Mom was in the living room, kneeling in front of our scrawny little tree. She was putting a few ornaments back on the branches. She smiled at me.

"Merry Christmas, Mom."

"Merry Christmas, Max."

There weren't any presents under the tree, but I didn't care.

We were happy anyway, and it was a beautiful day outside.

"Where's Dad?"

"He just went out to clear the snow off the car," my mother answered.

All of a sudden, we heard a noise in the stairwell. When the door opened, I almost passed out!

It was Santa Claus! The real Santa Claus! The red cap, the

belly, the bag, and the beard that looked like cotton wool!

"Ho! Ho! Ho! Hello, children! Ho! Ho! Ho!"

This was the first time we had ever seen Santa in our own home! We stood frozen in the middle of the living room, wide-eyed and mouths agape. I thought I was dreaming.

"This can't be. It's impossible. This isn't real!"

I looked more closely at Santa Claus and I recognized him. It was the Santa Claus from the mall! He went over to my sisters and gave them some crayons and colouring books.

Then he turned to me.

"Hello, Max! Ho! Ho! Ho!"

Strangely enough, he remembered my name. He reached into

his sack and pulled out a present for me. I opened it and shrieked with delight. It was the Flying Avenger costume!

"Merry Christmas! Ho! Ho! Ho! See you next year! You be good boys and girls!"

Santa Claus left and we jumped for joy around Mom. I had never been so excited.

I put on the jet boots and the silver mask. I slipped the magic ring onto my finger. My mother tied the red cape around my neck.

Now I was the Flying Avenger!

I flew through the house, my cape streaming in the wind. I was afraid of nothing. I was the strongest one in the world. I could have vanquished the

Venimous Mole, the Whizzing Saws, and Lava Man!

Suddenly, we heard another noise in the stairwell. The door opened and Dad came in.

"Dad! Dad! Where were you?"

"Uh, I just went down to the corner store ..."

"Santa Claus came! Santa Claus was here!"

I flew from one chair to the next, leaving a shining trail behind me. Suddenly I noticed something strange.

"Dad, you have a bit of cotton wool caught in your hair."

My mom brushed it off, and my dad turned as red as my cape. He looked down. He didn't know what to say. The bit of cotton wool looked just like Santa's beard.

I looked my father in the eye and I asked, “Dad, were you Santa Claus?”

Everyone fell silent. My mother and my sisters didn’t move. My father leaned towards me.

“Well, Max,” he said, “are you the Flying Avenger?”

I didn’t know how to answer him. In a way, I was the Flying Avenger, but I was still Max at the same time.

Then my mother cried, “The Flying Avenger is the son of Santa Claus!”

Afterword

Months have passed since Christmas and I'm still crazy about my costume. At night I fly through the sky, high above the rooftops. My red cape shimmers beautifully in the wind.

My magic ring gives me superhuman courage and strength. Nothing frightens me, not even the Winged Scorpion, or the Missile Shark, or the Carnivorous Frog!

I am the strongest one in the universe! We have spaghetti with meat sauce again. My little sisters are happy and laughing like before, and my mother is radiant. I should tell you that my father finally got a new job.

The Flying Avenger is looking

out for them. They can sleep soundly. When you are happy, it's like Christmas every day of the year.